Nora Hopper

Under Quicken Boughs

Nora Hopper

Under Quicken Boughs

ISBN/EAN: 9783337206864

Printed in Europe, USA, Canada, Australia, Japan

Cover: Foto ©Andreas Hilbeck / pixelio.de

More available books at **www.hansebooks.com**

Under Quicken Boughs

UNDER QUICKEN BOUGHS

DARK JOAN

BY NORA HOPPER

LONDON: JOHN LANE ·
THE BODLEY HEAD
NEW·YORK· GEORGE·RICH-
MOND·AND·CO· MDCCCXCVI

CONTENTS

CONTENTS

CONTENTS

The King of Ireland's Son

Now all away to Tir na n'Og are many roads that
    run,
But he has ta'en the longest lane, the King of Ire-
    land's son.

There's roads of hate, and roads of love, and many
    a middle way,
And castles keep the valleys deep where happy
    lovers stray—

Where Aongus goes there's many a rose burns red
    mid shadows dun,
No rose there is will draw his kiss, the King of
    Ireland's son.

And yonder where the sun is high Love laughs
    amid the hay,
But smile and sigh have passed him by, and never
    make delay.

And here (and O ! the sun is low !) they're glad for
    harvest won,
But naught he cares for wheat or tares, the King of
    Ireland's son !

And you have flung love's apple by, and I'm to
   pluck it yet :
But what are fruits of gramarye with druid dews
   beset ?

Oh, what are magic fruits to him who meets the
   Lianan sidhe ?
Or hears athwart the distance dim Fionn's horn
   blow drowsily ?

The star is yours to win or lose, and me the dusk
   has won,
He follows after shadows, the King of Ireland's son.

Silk o' the Kine

(To Coulson Kernahan)

Silk o' the Kine, it's long you've strayed away
Into the meadows thro' the twilight gray :
And though we stand and call when night is near
And draws the weary cattle homeward here,
You never come : nor any pishogue may
Bring you to us at dawning o' the day,
        Silk o' the Kine.

Manannan drives his cattle from the sea
At sundown : but no heart to watch have we
For thinking on our own that's strayed so far
Beyond the shining of the hunter's star :
For thinking on you, and your silk coat fine,
        Silk o' the Kine !

We have no heart to heed the thrush's song,
The hound's deep note, the blackbird's fluting
    long—
(The song Fionn loved at Derrycarn of streams,)
Our hearts are wandering with you in our dreams,
Nor can we turn our sorrow into song—
My grief, my grief ! we've missed you over-long,
        Silk o' the Kine !

Eireag

(BEAUTY)

EIREAG goeth by dale and down
With a garland of furze for all her crown :
      Eireag, Eireag !

She goes by down and she goes by dale,
For lack of sorrow her face is pale.

Tree after tree at her feet casts down,
Oak-leaves and beech-leaves, yellow and brown.

From pool and river the sheogues rise,
Dreaming, they follow her dreaming eyes.

At last they come to the open sea,
And Manan gathers them greedily :

So long, so low do the merrows call,
And Manan gathers them, one and all.

They followed thee, Eireag, a weary while,
Canst not weep if thou wilt not smile ?

Canst not weep for them, drowned and dead,
Lost for the love of thy dear black head?

Lost in the smother of drowning seas,
Never a tear have thine eyes for these?

Lost and left in the bitter brine,
Life of thy lovers, and death of thine,
　　　Eireag, Eireag!

Finvarragh

(To William Butler Yeats)

I am the King of Faery :
 A thousand years ago
My elfin mother bore me
 Between the snow and snow.
My elfin mother bore me
 —Lightly, as fairies may—
To rule a doubtful country
 Between the dusk and day.

I am the King of Faery :
 And wise I am, and old,
And of my fairy wisdom
 A thousand hands take hold.
But those that seek my helping
 Are glad, for all their care.
My thousand years of wisdom
 Lie dark upon my hair.

I am the King of Faery :
 And none there is so gay
Among my gentle people
 That dance the dews away.

I am the King of Faery
    And none there is so sad,
Though Una is my lady
    And Aodh my serving-lad.

I am the King of Faery,
    And I, and all my kin,
May neither weep for sorrow,
    May neither serve nor sin.
But we shall fade as dewdrops
    That morning sun has dried :
So serve us who have served you,
    And set your kind doors wide.

Vagrants

AND first the Night, lost in her wild black hair,
Came crooning down the valleys to Kenmare,
   Crooning an old song lost the raths amid,
      Far fallen from love and grace,
   Since days when first the darkness Oscar hid
      And covered Niam's face :
Night, moving slowly, lost in visions sweet
And all the cabins listening for her feet.

And after her came Dawn,
As swift and wild and shy as any fawn.
A glimmer of grey eyes, and moonlit hair,
     A flutter in the air—
A cry of wakening birds, that hardly may
Believe so near the day :
Her feet went by like shadows ; from her track
    You saw the dreams draw back.

Then Day came, woman grown, and gravely sweet,
With steady eyes and undelaying feet :
She had no time for dreams, nor yet for song,
    For all day long
Barefooted, mid the children born of her,
She worked among the fields a harvester.

Dear Black Head

Dear Black Head, will you go with me
Where the Tir na n'Og shines mistily?
Climbing the mountains or sailing the sea,
Dear Black Head, will you go with me?

On seas uncharted though we set sail
I will not fail you though all things fail;
I'd drown light-hearted your love to be,
Dear Black Head, will you go with me?

Avourneen deelish, your dear black head
Shall know no sorrow until I'm dead:
Your borrow in sorrow or shame I'll be,
Dear Black Head, if you'll go with me.

And till the Islands of Youth we find
Oh, I'll be faithful and you'll be kind —
Your heart of gold shall my castle be,
Dear Black Head, if you'll go with me!

Ma Bouchaleen Bwee

(My Yellow-haired Lad)

Ma bouchaleen bwee, and ma bouchaleen bwee,
It's I would go with you wherever you be :
I'd climb the high hills and I'd sail the salt sea
If I might go with you, ma bouchaleen bwee.

Most dear and most green are the fair hills of Eri,
But on steeper hillsides my feet would not weary :
My feet on the ice and the snowfield might be
If you climbed beside me, ma bouchaleen bwee.

If you were in exile, whatever winds blew,
It's I would be houseless and homeless with you :
My breast for your fair head a pillow should be,
And my heart for your castle, ma bouchaleen bwee !

With sorrow before and with danger behind,
I'd follow you, heeding nor weather nor wind :
So kind and so faithful and patient I'd be,
If I might go with you, ma bouchaleen bwee.

A Song of Three Sisters

(Minnie, Edith, and Alice)

White rose and red, red rose and white,
Grew in my garden plain to sight,
And by them, tall and pale to see
There grew a plant of honesty.

But few so wise there were to see
Eyes shining from the honesty,
Kind eyes, filled full of hope and care,
Midmost the shadow of brown hair.

And few or none might see a star,
(Less bright than those that toss afar
Their golden cressets) softly part
The leaves that fold the red rose-heart.

And few or none might see—as I
When slept red rose and honesty—
Gray wings from out the green leaves grow
And rock the white rose to and fro.

Fire and Snow

"What of the night, colleen, what of the night?"
Oh, fires are red and the snows are white:
But on one dear hearth that I used to know
The fire is quenched with the drifted snow.

"What bird is it, colleen, that cries so shrill?"
'Tis I; and I cry for a kind voice still—
For a kind hand slipped from my clinging hold,
For my place in a heart that to-night is cold.

"What of the night, colleen, what of the night?"
Oh, never a star dares show its light,
But wildfire signals to ships at sea—
And Miscann Many's the fire for me.

One may sit by the wild-fire, and half forget
The hands that parted, the lips that met:
One may warm one's grief there; for deathly cold
Is the heart that has never a pain to hold.

"What pain is it, colleen, you'd win again
By the fire that's quenched not of wind or rain?
Why sit you silent the while you spin,
As if your sorrow were half a sin?"

What use of wailing ? more use to spin,
And dearest is sorrow that's half a sin—
And the ghostly feet that I hear on the stair,
Oh, they must walk soft though my heart go bare.

Oh, mother, mother, one thing alone
Keeps shut my lips that would fain make moan,
It is that alone in the night I go
And dree my weird betwixt snow and snow.

Oh, sea-blue eyes of you, yellow head,
You passed ere the flowers on the thorn were dead :
And I give God thanks, though the ways be white,
That His snows fall only on me to-night.

Dark Joan

As old as Time is, as cold as a stone,
I go on my journey, Dark Joan, Dark Joan.
My cap is made of a quicken-leaf,
And withered it is, my grief, my grief!
My eyes are dark, but they see the soul,
And where Time reads half I can read the whole.

As sad as Death is, I go on my way
And sow, though for harvest I must not stay:
By the Good Folk's passing my face is fanned,
Yet I must not dance in their idle band:
In the raths I hear them, my kindly kin,
But the sorrowful cabins they call me in.

A Charm

Nor sweet with wild honey from combs o' the Shee,
But bitter with sorrow 's this song made o' me :
Yet my song, acushla, sweet to no maid's ear,
I lay it upon you to heed and to hear.

Not red are my apples, nor mellow my wine :
In shadow they ripened, these apples of mine :
Of my wine, acushla, and my fruits unsweet,
I lay it upon you to drink and to eat.

Bees that stored my honey, fruits my life has fed,
Charm you hither, hither, ere the spell he said,
Though the Shee in pity made you deaf and dumb,
I lay it upon you to hear, and to come.

Nóra Crióna.

You were like a lily on a grave,
        Nóra Crióna !
White and fair and frail : too frail to brave
Autumn's winds and winter's shrouding snow
For the sake of one that slept below.
Now no winds you fear, nor summer heat,
Snow, nor stinging sleet, Nóra Crióna !

You were like a lily on a grave,
        Nóra Crióna !
Golden heart and silver soul you gave
Us, who gave you Sorrow to your maid
Care, to watch you in your silken bed :
O'er you lilies keep their watch to-night—
Lilies far less white, Nóra Crióna !

You were like a lily on a grave,
        Nóra Crióna !
Now your sister-lilies hold and have
What we fain would break our hearts to keep :
We that scorned your waking, grudge your sleep .
We would kiss your lily to a rose
But sleep holds you close, Nóra Crióna !

You were like a lily on a grave,
        Nóra Crióna !
Life had naught to bring you, but Death gave
Fairest fruit and finest flower of all !
Oh, your going left in bower and hall
Fewer smiles and many secret tears,
Ay, and shaken spears, Nóra Crióna !

A Song of the Sword

It was welded in fires of Eve's own kindling, and
    tempered in tears that Lilith wept,
Fires that were tended of Dhoul and Druid and
    Gods that woke while the others slept.
And the fire was hallowed with prayers and sighing
    of saints that took it for sleeping-place,
With life unborn and with life undying, with
    prayers unanswered and granted grace.

The fire was watched of the dark Fomoroh, from
    wistful twilight to windy dawn,
De Dananns fed it with quicken-branches, the wild
    Shee came from their dancing lawn !
They sang wild songs to the red fire's flashing, they
    sang to the red fire's falling glow,
And ours are the fire and the sword it welded, but
    free for us now the wild songs go.

The fire's forlorn of the wayward singing, but rich
    it kindles and richer now
By crimson stones that the dark Fomoroh stripped
    for its pleasure, from breast and brow.

C

It called for wood and we brought it quicken, it
    cried for dew and we brought it blood,
We sent pale colleens its flame to strengthen, to
    tread the deeps of its crimson flood.

We gave it blood and we gave it blossoms, gold
    coins and amber and golden hair,
Kings' daughters fed with their flower its hunger,
    and the sons of kings were its playthings fair.
Its eager arms for a Danann princess reached out
    not long in a vain desire,
It has given the sword to be our servant, and we
    are the servants of the fire.

To a Poet

AND have you passed the druid gates
  Where arméd Angels stand
And found the house where Kathleen waits
  To heal the thorn-pricked hand,
And wreath with ivy leaves the head
  Long bared to wind and rain,
Ere hand and head to the Rose that's red
  Be vowed, and hers remain?

And have you breathed the very air
  Full of the Rose's breath?
Have you beheld her strange and fair
  Yourself untouched of death?
How comes it, then, so bold you are
  That you can bide the pain
Of seeing her grow faint and far,
  And earth your own again?

Yet lack of yours is gain of ours
  And we are very fain
To see you here 'mid earthly flowers,
  Tended by mortal men.
Stay here awhile for kindness' sake,
  And sing the Rose a space
Until, like you, our bonds we break,
  And see her very face.

Gray Sails

(To John Lane)

What do you look for, 'twixt dusk and gloaming,
White sails going or gray sails homing ?

Sunset turns white sails red in the bay,
Gloaming finds not the sails of gray.

Patched and rotten the gray sails were,
White sails gleam in the sunset air.

Under the white sails hearts are gay,
Sorrow sailed with the sails of gray.

Sorrow for pilot and skipper Sin—
What if the gray sails never came in.

Peril of ship and soul might be—
What if they sailed to a quiet sea ?

Safe from danger of rock and blast—
Where sails of gray might be furled at last ?

The red wind out of the East blows on
O'er white sails going and gray sails gone—

Somewhere or other the red wind sees
Quiet harbours where ride at ease

Ships that were stormbound far away,
Ships with white sails and ships with gray.

Hush your keen in the windy gloaming,
In that good harbour gray sails are homing.

The Parting of the Ways

WHAT was the dream in your eyes grown dim when
    the dawn awoke, and at night's gates cried,
And a billow of red flushed overhead the faces of
    dead stars swept aside?
What dream did you dream that you turned from
    him that loved you best o' the world, asthore,
That you turned your head on your weary bed, and
    no word said as you passed Death's door?

Which way to follow by hill and hollow, and on,
    and over the green world's rim?
By the Land of Youth where kind words are sooth,
    and for bitter truth no eyes grow dim?
Or in darker ways, where the end is haze and the
    traveller strays amid fields forlorn,
Where in thorny brakes for their light loves' sakes
    poor lovers wander, and see no morn?

Were you sinner or saint, blue eyes and faint gold
    hair hanging down on your breast of snow?
Shall I find in heaven your soul forgiven, or seek
    unshriven where the four winds blow,

Where rain is red, and kind Hope lies dead on a
    golden bed in ghostly state,
And none may borrow of joy or sorrow the gift
    whereby they may pass the gate?

Come back and say where you dwell to-day, my
    colleen oge and my colleen bawn :
If I must go where the light burns low, and never
    a night is friends with dawn?
Or upwards climb to the steeps sublime, where even
    the hills near by are blue?
Which way will I take for my storeen's sake?
    which way, agra, must I follow you?

Soontree

(A Lullaby)

My joy and my grief, go sleep and gather
Dreams from the tree where the dreams hang low,
Rounder than apples, and sweeter than honey,
All to delight you, ma creevin cno !

My joy, fill your dear hands full of roses,
And gather lilies that stand a-row :
Pull rush and reed with the Shee's fair children,
But eat not, drink not, ma creevin cno !

You may not taste of the cups of honey,
You may not taste of the wine blood-red,
Of the mead and the wine he drank, your father,
And the next night's rain wept your father, dead.

Reach up to the star that hangs the lowest,
Tread down the drift of the apple-blow,
Ride your ragweed horse to the Isle of Nobles,
But the Shee's wine drink not, ma creevin cno !
                    Shoheen, shoheen, shoheen sho !

Iseult of Ireland

" ISEULT " and " Iseult,"
   " Iseult " all day,
Yammer and cry the gulls that fly
   Tintagel way.

Tristram and Iseult—
   Ivy and rose,
Twist there and make for old sake's sake
   The knot Love knows.

Ivy o'er Iseult
   Clambers and clings :
The wind that blows Tristram's rose
   Folds there his wings.

Larks over Iseult
   Sweet service say,
And lovers' feet are fain to meet
   Tintagel way.

High over Iseult's,
   Though his grave be,
There lies a doom on Arthur's tomb
   That none may see.

" Tristram and Iseult "
Love sets to rhyme :
Shall they not rise pure in Love's eyes
In his good time ?

The Dinny Math

(To W. B. Y.)

WE are the gentle people :
   The passing dust we are,
With gusty laughter blowing
      Near and far.
We are the gentle people,
   Nor deal in praise or blame,
But we stand before your sorrow,
   And we stand behind your shame.

We are the gentle people,
And soft our music's blown
When kindly hearts that loved us
Are passing from their own.
We are the gentle people,
And gently draw away
The light feet to our dancing
Night and day.

We are the gentle people,
   And though our toll we take
Of milk and meal and water—
      For old sake's sake

Ye grudge us not, who grudge not
  To watch your folded kine,
To bless the wheels and the pillows
        And the lace-threads fine.

We are the gentle people,
  Mavrone, and we shall pass
Even as the dew, that Morning
  Dries from the short green grass.
Oh, the dew returns at twilight,
  But not so we—
We shall pass like wind, so be ye kind
  To the passing Shee.

Gold Song

" Gold of butterflies, gold of bees,
   Gold of ragweeds and golden seas ;
   Gold on gorses for kissing's sake,
   Which of these will you touch and take,
          Moirín, Moirín ? "

Golden butterfly's not for me,
   I'll ha' none o' the golden bee :
   My heart of gold shall not beat nor break,
   Though I love the gorses for kissing's sake,
          Mother, Mother !

" Then rest you merry, through heat and cold,
   Sweet lips of cherry, sweet heart of gold ;
   Yet Gold-Heart surely shall come some day
   To cry for gray wings to fly away,
          Moirín, Moirín ! "

May Eve

THERE'S a crying at my window, and a hand upon
    my door,
And a stir among the yarrow that's fading on the
    floor :
The voice cries at my window, the hand at my door
    beats on,
But if I heed and answer them, sure, hand and voice
    are gone.

You would not heed my calling once, and now why
    would I hear ?
You would not hold my wistful hand, but let it fall,
    my dear :
You would not give me word or look, but went your
    silent way,
Oh, wirrasthrue, dumb mouth of you that had so
    much to say.

Be still, my dear : I heed, I hear, but cannot help
    you now,
The rose is dead that was so red, and snow's upon
    her bough.
Be still, be still a little while, for I shall surely come
And kiss the sorrow from your eyes, and from your
    kind lips dumb.

Be patient now, avourneen ! you may not lift the
  latch :
Go hence : the wind is bitter cold that whistles
  through the thatch.
The wind is cold, and I am old, but you're young
  and fair to see,
And my heart turns to you night and day, my fair
  love leaving me !

Wild Geese

Wild Geese, wild Geese, where are you going?
The mist's before you, behind's the rain:
The red east wind thro' your plumes is blowing—
When will it blow you back home again?

Wild Geese, wild Geese, where you are going
My heart goes also, and fain would flee
Farther away where the Hunter's glowing,
But Miscann Many's the light for me.

After the wildfire I must follow,
Tho' the way is dark where I set my feet—
While you fly hence amid crying hollow,
The wind's long keen, and the lash of sleet.

Good speed, wild Geese, and a truce to sighing!
Fair fall your way over wind and wave,
Till I awaken, and hear you flying
Over and over my bogland grave.

Ceol-Sidhe

THERE never was any music
In the golden throat of a bird,
More fine and clear than the piping
That in dreams I heard
Cry through the Heart Lake's rushes,
And falter and fade away,
Like odours of thyme one crushes
      In the heat of the day.

There never was any piping
So sweet and tender and gay,
It came like the wind, and lightly
      It blew away—
It laughed and it grew not weary,
It sighed and was sweeter yet,
It sang for the hope of Eri
      And her heavy fret.

There never was any piping
So merry and none so sad,
For it sang of a far green island
      Where, scarlet-clad,

All under the druid quicken,
Wild dancers gather and go,
And under the oaks, unstricken,
   Feeds Saav, the doe.

And when silence took the piping,
"It's O to be there," I cried,
"To dance with no thought of grieving
   For joy that died—
To dance, and be never weary
 For night or day,
With the kindliest folk of Eri
   Till the dew's away.
Sweet, sweet is the twilight dancing,
 Not sweet is the homespun day."
But the dawn through the rushes glancing
   Drove my dream away.

A Drowned Man's Sweetheart

FIACHRA, Fiachra,
  Call all your waves to heel :
The moon is white as death to-night,
  The air is sharp to feel.
My Ulick's sailing far to-night—
  You kind, kind folk that are
To fade away like dew at day,
  Light up your evening star.

Fiachra, Fiachra,
  Keep guard down all the coast,
For sure am I that I would die
  If Ulick's boat were lost.
Oh, show the rocks and show the shore,
  And show the open bay ;
I'm blind with tears for all the years
  Since Ulick sailed away.

Fiachra, Fiachra,
  Where Manan's table's set
Under the sea he sits maybe,
  And dreams of Aileen yet.

'Tell him she's wed and Terence dead,
  And lone I sit and spin—
In Mary's name, from the sea-flame
  And sea-dusk, call him in !

Fiachra, Fiachra;
  Are all the faces fair
Under the sea, and merrily
  Rings all the laughter there ?
Mavrone ! for O my roses go,
  My singing voice is broke—
So bid him stay for ever away
  Among the kind sea-folk.

Over the Hills and Far Away

(To E. Nesbit)

Last night, last night, in the dark o' the moon
Into my dreams slid a faery tune . . .
It slew the dreams that I dreamed of him,
With its moonshine music, faint and dim.
What tune should the fairy pipers play
But "Over the Hills and Far Away?"

The music called to my idle feet,
And O! the music was wild and sweet:
I left my dreams and my lonely bed,
And followed afar where the music led—
And never a tune did the pipers play
But "Over the Hills and Far Away."

Over the hills and far away,
What love has tenderer words to say?
Love that lifteth or bows the head,
Love that liveth or love that's dead?
Hills that are far away are fair,
And I followed the ghost of my lover there.

We danced all night in a silent band,
I and my lover, hand in hand:
We danced, nor knew till the dew was dry
That deep slept Donat and lone slept I —
We took no thought of the coming day
Over the hills and far away.

My eyes are blind with the growing light,
And O my grief! that the day was night—
For my heart is broke, for my lover's eyes,
And all day long in my ears there cries
The tune of the fairy pipes that play
"Over the Hills and Far Away."

The Passing of the Shee

And did you meet them riding down
A mile away from Galway town?
Wise childish eyes of Irish gray,
You must have seen them, too, to-day.

And did you hear wild music blow
All down the boreen, long and low,
The tramp of ragweed-horses' feet,
And Una's laughter, wild and sweet?

Oh, once *I* met them riding down
A hillside far from Galway town:
But not alone I walked that day
To hear the fairy pipers play—

They lighted down, the kindly Shee,
They builded palace-walls for me—
They built me bower, they built me bawn,
Ganconagh, Banshee, Leprechaun.

They builded me a chamber fair,
Roofed in with music, walled with air,
And in its garden, fair to sight,
Grew wallflowers, windflowers, brown and white.

Bouchaleen bwee, if you should see
One riding with the happy Shee
One with blue eyes and yellow hair,
Less light of heart than many there—

Ah, tell him that *I'm* seeking still
Our fairy hold by fairy hill—
Following the fairy pipes that play
Over the hills and far away.

Red Clay

You shall not meet in kindness
      Any more:
I strike your loves with blindness
  And shut a stubborn door,
That will not open, Mauryeen, at your cry:
That will not open, Terence, till you die.
I have the bearing of my own heart's pain,
  Dear pain that Terence gave:
But here I softly lay betwixt you twain
      Clay from a grave.

So small a grave lies yonder,
      Inishkea
Holds it ; and sea-gulls wander
  There from the open sea.
Cry out upon the sea-gulls from your door,
Mauryeen, they bode no good so far inshore.
The sea-gulls heard you, Terence ; and the sea
Surely some day shall fling you back to me,
      And then, maybe,
Mauryeen will not desire you, dear black head,
      A drowned man, dead.

You shall not meet, my storeen,
      At dawn nor dark—
Crossing the shadowy boreen
      Where the red lark
Cries to his hid wife from the windy sky,
Deeming *his* love at least shall never die.
I cast between your hands that shall not meet
  'To serve nor yet to save,
I cast red clay between your wandering feet,
      From my child's grave.

A Song of Four Winds

THE gray wind out of the West
　Is sighing and making moan,
For a noinin's silver crest
　In the hay-swathes overthrown.
Like the heart in a dying breast,
　It flutters, making its moan,
The gray wind out of the West.

The black wind out of the North
　Blows loud, like a cry of war :
Its voice goes gallantly forth
　In fields where the spearsmen are :
To them is its voice not worth
　Wild music of any star ?
The black wind out of the North.

The white wind out of the South,
　It makes not for war nor peace :
"Tis the breath of a colleen's mouth,
　Yet it flutters the willow-trees :
It burns men's souls with drouth,
　Then fills their souls with ease :
The white wind out of the South.

The red wind out of the East—
  What word can a harper say
Of the wind that blows from the feast,
  And blows men into the fray :
It will not stay for the priest,
  For the Host it will not stay—
The red wind blowing out of the East,
  The wind of the Judgment Day.

Irish Ivy

Ivy of Ireland in my garden grows
Beside the foxglove that the wild bee knows,
More dear to me than lavender or rose.

Gray moths about it flit, and gold wasps hum :
The bees salute it softly as they come :
The east wind loiters by it, and is dumb—

Or whispers very lightly of green rings,
And hollow raths, and fairy-peopled springs,
And buried days when Boholaun had wings :

And rode amid the unforgotten Shee.
Or the west wind comes, laughing, from the sea,
And tells the youngest leaves of days to be,

When Eri's grievous wound is healed, and she
Shall lift her gracious head, and, smiling, see
Her children coming crowned about her knee.

Ivy of Ireland, is the promise clear ?
You climb towards the light 'twixt hope and fear.
But would to God the day we wait were here !

Song of the Fomoroh

Who dare set bounds to the Red Wind,
   The East Wind in his wrath?
Lo! we have bitted and bridled him,
   And turned him from his path:
From the waves that beat we have called his feet
   To the long grass of the rath.

He hath heard our call through his tempest fall,
   And he maketh no delay,
Though the house of the Dawn's his homestead,
   Yet there he will not stay:
And the voice that compels his coming
   Is neither of night nor day.

The voice blows out of the twilight,
   As thistle-drift is blown,
It's light, and tender, and merry,
   And the seeds that its call has sown
Are sin, and desire, and sorrow,
   And the world hears, and moves on.

From his wings we've ta'en the scarlet stain,
   The red plumes from his crest:

We've snatched from his hands the sea-pinks
 Wherewith his cliffs were drest :
We have fed our fire to heart's desire,
 With the bird that beat in his breast.

Ay, we ha' bridled the red East Wind
 With none to say him Nay—
With his heart's blood red our fires we fed
 That the sword might be swift to slay,
And the ashes at last to his own wind cast,
 That they might be blown away.

For we are the dark Formoroh,
 And sore we travail that ye
May cast off care, and grow strong and fair,
 And still our bondsmen be :
We shall enter in your souls, our kin,
 And who shall our slaying see ?

The Strangers

THEY bought her, not with Irish knife,
　But with their Danish gold :
They brought her from her father's hall,
　From faces kind to faces cold
　　In her new lord's hold.
They laid strange hands on her joyous life,
　And bade the bird in her breast to sing
An altered song with a folded wing :
　And the Irish maid was a Danish wife
In the Strangers' Forts (*and she heard, she heard*
　All night the cry of an alien bird
That would not sing for the Strangers
　Who dwelt in Donegal).

They took her over running water,
　And loosed our kindly chain :
And Danish son and Danish daughter
　She bare unto her Dane.
She sang their songs, and in the singing
　　Her childish tunes forgot :
　And she remembered not
The kindlier hearts that years were bringing
　　Joy and pain
That were none of hers, though deep the gladness

And keen the pain—
For she knew no grief but the near-hand sadness
  That vexed the Dane :
And her joy was the joy of an outland lord,
And gay she sat at the outland board
  In the highest hall,
(But it would not sing for a Danish call,
The bird in her breast that must make its nest
In the Strangers' Forts, with the Strangers
  That dwelt in Donegal).

She bore him three fair daughters,
And one tall son, whose name
The Danish minstrels lifted up,
Even as one lifts a golden cup
Filled to the lips with fame.
Then over the shadowy waters
She saw Hy-Brasail gleam—
And she laid her down on her carven bed,
 Most white, and fair, and sweet to see
As a dream remembered piteously
 When we grow too old to dream.
 And " Being but dead "—
 She said, " I bid you carry me
Like a maiden back to my own country,
 Not like a wife long-wed.
Take off my girdle and jewels all,
My shining keys, and my Irish knife :
Bid my maids go at my daughter's call,
And my heathen thrall
May serve my son, for my toils are done,
  And no other care
I have save this, that ye bear me back
  On the homeward track,

With a strait blue gown for my only wear,
With folded fingers and unbound hair,
    As I was ne'er a wife,
For I cannot sleep, being dead—
In the Strangers' Forts, with the strangers
    That dwell in Donegal."
(And dead she lay, and above her bed
A bird's voice cried, till the light o'erhead
    Grew dark to the evenfall.
And its cry was the cry of the Strangers
    That dwelt in Donegal.)

Now, her alien kin, and her alien mate,
    We held deep in hate :
    We that were once her own,
We from whose griefs her heart had grown,
    And whose joys, mavrone,
Passed by her door—and she had not known.
We that by cold hearths sat alone
    When her thread was shorn
By envious hands of a Danish Norn.
And, mavrone, mavrone, but we liked it ill
That they did her dying will :
And bore her homewards as she had said
With empty hands and unveiled head,
    Like a maiden still.
And we hated more when they raised no wail
    Above her cairn,
Standing dumb and stern,
Drinking "Godspeed" in her burial-ale
While our women shrieked ; and with faces pale
Stood and cursed our mountain kerne.
And now we are sad, for our hate is shed
Abroad on the wings of the wind, and dead

As Eivir, as Eivir.   And home to his hall
    Scathlessly goes the Dane.
And the cock we had reared, the cock that's red,
    Crows not on his castle-wall.
(But the bird, the bird we loved best of all,
It sits and sings in his lonely hall,
    Mavrone! for her bosom-bird
And its singing voice we have not heard
    O'er her grave in the Holy Isle:
Nor yet in the dusk o'er her maiden bed,
In the hold where she was born,
It sings, by night or morn.
But it sings most sweet and clear
For her Danish kin to hear:
And its song is sad, and its song is glad,
Like a sigh that grows to a smile.)
For she loved us both, but death turns love cold,
And they bring us back our dead to hold,
So they loved her best, the Strangers
    That dwell in Donegal.

Wicklow Hills

(To W. Y. Fletcher)

I heard the noise of fairy pipes complaining all
    night long
What time the skies were empty of cloud and star
    and song.
I heard the noise of fairy pipes complaining far
    away,
High up among the Wicklow Hills till dawning o'
    the day.

Oh, far was I from Wicklow Hills, and yet I saw
    and knew
Beneath the feet of dancers there how shone the
    druid dew :
My feet were moving to the tune that fairy pipers
    play
High up among the Wicklow Hills till dawning o'
    the day.

My dead love danced all night with me among the
    deathless Shee,
And we were young and gay again together, I and
    he—

Though he was dead in Devenish, and I was far
  away,
We danced all night on Wicklow Hills till dawning
  o' the day.

It's O the kindly hands I grasped, the kindly eyes
  I knew—
It's O to greet the dancing feet to-night amid the
  dew :
But the pipes are still, and never a hill I see but's
  far away
And I turn my head on a widowed bed, at dawning
  o' the day.

Saav's Lament

O LITTLE fawn, it's long you've strayed away,
 It's near the break of day:
Long I've been seeking you by hill and hollow
My voice and feet will you not rise and follow,
  O little fawn?

O little fawn, they say a sheogue met you
 Long since and far away —
Oh! hearken now my calling, nor delay!
 It's near the break of day,
When fawn and doe should sleep in the long grass
Take heed, for there is many a darkling pass
Betwixt us, many snares that will beset you,
  O little fawn!

O little fawn, there are no grasses growing
 More sweet to crop than these:
Not any sown round Niam's palaces.
Arise, O little fawn, leave thy gold prison,
And come to me ere yet the sun is risen:
Ere yet the red wind on his way is going,
  O little fawn!

O little fawn, although you have forgotten
    These many, many years :
Although beneath her spells your eyes have grown
    Unused to tears,
Yet, fear me, Niam, since I seek my own—
My own will come to me : my first-begotten,
       My little fawn !

The Grey Fog

THERE's a grey fog over Dublin of the curses,
It blinds my eyes, mavrone ; and stops my breath,
And I travel slow that once could run the swiftest,
And I fear ere I meet Mauryeen I'll meet Death.

There's a grey fog over Dublin of the curses,
And a grey fog dogs my footsteps as they go,
And its long and sore to tread, the road to Connaught.
Is it fault of brogues or feet I fare so slow ?

There's a grey fog over Dublin of the curses,
But the Connaught wind will blow it from my way,
And a Connaught girl will kiss it from my memory,
If the Death that walks beside me will delay.

(There's a grey fog over Dublin of the curses,
And no wind comes to break its stillness deep :
And a Connaughtman lies on the road to Connaught,
And Mauryeen will not kiss him from his sleep—
    Ululu !)

The Cuckoo Sings in the Heart of Winter

THE cuckoo sings in the heart of winter,
And all for Mauryeen he tunes his song ;
How Mauryeen's hair is the honey's colour
(He sings of her all the winter long !)

Her long loose hair's of the honey's colour,
The wild sweet honey that wild bees make,
The sun herself is ashamed before her,
The moon is pale for her gold cool's sake.

She bound her hair of the honey's colour,
With flowers of yarrow and quicken green :
And now one binds it with leaves of willow,
And cypress lies where my head has been.

Now robins sing beside Pastheen's doorway,
And wrens for bounty that Grania gave :
The cuckoo sings in the heart of winter,
He sings all day beside Mauryeen's grave.

Roisin Dubh

EVERYONE knows that a rose will fade,
    (Sure I knew, too !)
So why would I be a whit dismayed
    When you died, Roisin dubh ?
For a day and a night and a morrow
    The bloom of you—
Then death : and what use of sorrow
    For a rose, Roisin dubh ?

Yet, little black rose, so dear you were,
    So sweet you grew,
And your stem is sad now you are not there,
    And your leaves, Roisin dubh !
O little black rose, my soul I'd give,
    (My body, too !)
For a day, for an hour, that you might live
    On your bush, Roisin dubh !

Sweet, sweet, till the world was glad for you,
    And kinder, too—
Now your bush and your world are sad for you,
    Roisin dubh !

The Hill-Winds

THE hill-winds coming, the hill-winds going,
   They have no care for my heavy fret :
I lay my face in the long grass growing,
   And dream of Moirin, and half forget
That never a wind in the world is blowing
   Her thoughts to my heart that loves her yet.

The hill-winds going, the hill-winds coming,
   I take no heed of them all day long—
Though I lie in their heart from dawn to gloaming,
   And hark the bees where the clovers throng :
And, O wild bees, that you'd hush your humming :
   What comfort is there in comb or song ?

The hill-winds fly without care or cumber,
   And scent of bean-fields they bring to me,
Where magic flowers without name or number
   Are sending dreams where sad sleepers be :
But none so deep as the honeyed slumber
   Of Moirin drowned in the Ictian Sea.

Four Sisters

In Connaught and Leinster
  Tears wait for me,
But I dwell merrily
  Here by the sea.
My kirtle's gold-bordered,
  Gold tires my hair,
And red quicken-berries
  That Oscar once bare.

In Connaught my mother
  Sits by her door,
And calls her lost children
  Over and o'er.
A high hall of Leinster
  Shuts in from me,
Maive, Eily, Maire,
  Mairé the Shee.

Maive she has yellow hair
  Softer than silk :
Eily has hazel eyes
  And skin like milk.

Mairé's hair, chaffer-black,
  Hangs to her knee—
Eyes gray and bright as swords,
  Mairé the Shee.

Eily sings merrily
  All the day long,
Mairé spins wearily
  To Eily's song.
Black threads of sin she spins,
  Red threads of blame,
White threads and yellow threads,
  Love : death : and shame.

Which did he dearest hold,
  Mairé the Shee,
Who sent him down to death
  In the gray sea !
Eily his first beloved,
  Or Maive he wed ?
Or I whom once he crowned
  With berries red ?

Deelish !

DEELISH, Deelish, my eyes are darkened
  All for the light in your eyes grown dim :
Because of the words my ears have hearkened,
  Mute falls the music of prayer and hymn :
Good days are over with you, my lover—
  You're cold : let the warm world sink or swim !

Deelish, Deelish, where you lie lonely
  Do you start and listen for me to come—
Morning and midnight waiting only
  Till my steps silence the wild bees' hum ?
Bees, go on singing, your honey bringing—
  Comfort my lover where he lies dumb.

Deelish, Deelish, my gown I'll gather
  Full of heather and canna white ;
Walk alone where we walked together—
  And come to you ere the fall of night.
No priest will bless me, but you will kiss me,
  Deelish, and will not our dreams be light ?

The Sorrow of the Women

THE sorrow of the women, and the sorrow
  Drawn up like shining fishes from the seas
In all our nets: the griefs that grow together
  In sun and rainy weather
Like mosses gray on shadowy apple-trees;
  Like mosses gray: nor wither
When rose and sloe and lily dare not stay.
  For griefs are sturdy, and they hold together
  When thorns forget their May.
And who shall lift the doubt from off To-morrow
  And give us peace?
The darkness from To-day: and bid it cease—
  The sorrow of the women, and the sorrow?

Even he, who goes the way
  That is not known of any summer day:
Who passes the Wind's Height, the Marshes Yellow
With none for faring-fellow.
Who hears the Three Waves roaring after him,
And looks not back, but onward to the dim
Country where love and terror are not known,
But weeds and blossoms are together sown.

Yet there shall he find Terror, if he choose,
And Love, both bound in chains that he must loose :
And one shall be his own.
Hence to the Shee's dim country ; seek and find
Death chained, Love blind :
 Seek thou, and find
If Death be fair at all, or Love be kind ?
 Loose them, and let them be ;
 Follow them home, and see
The women bless another friend than thee :
 And thou shalt be our borrow.
(The sorrow of the women, and the sorrow.)

The Dark Man

Rose o' the world, she came to my bed
And changed the dreams of my heart and head :
For joy of mine she left grief of hers
And garlanded me with a crown of furze.

Rose o' the world, they go out and in,
And watch me dream, and my mother spin :
And they pity the tears on my sleeping face
While my soul's away in a faery place.

Rose o' the world, they have words galore,
And wide's the swing of my mother's door :
And soft they speak of my darkened eyes,
But what do they know, who are all so wise ?

Rose o' the world, the pain you give
Is worth all days that a man may live :
Worth all shy prayers that the colleens say
On the night that darkens the wedding-day.

Rose o' the world, what man would wed
When he might dream of your face instead ?
Might go to his grave with the blessed pain
Of hungering after your face again ?

Rose o' the world, they may talk their fill,
For dreams are good, and my life stands still
While their lives' red ashes the gossips stir,
But my fiddle knows: and *I* talk to her.

The Fairy Music

(To Katharine Tynan)

There's many feet on the moor to-night, and they
    fall so light as they turn and pass,
So light and true that they shake no dew from the
    featherfew and the Hungry grass.
I drank no sup and I broke no crumb of their food,
    but dumb at their feast sat I,
For their dancing feet and their piping sweet, now
    I sit and greet till I'm like to die.

Oh kind, kind folk, to the words you spoke I shut
    my ears and I would not hear,
And now all day what my own kin say falls sad and
    strange on my careless ear—
For I'm listening, listening, all day long to a fairy
    song that is blown to me,
Over the broom and the canna's bloom, and I know
    the doom of the Ceol-Sidhe.

I take no care now for bee or bird, for a voice I've
    heard that is sweeter yet,
My wheel stands idle : at death or bridal apart I
    stand and my prayers forget.

When Ulick speaks of my wild-rose cheeks, and his
    kind love seeks out my heart that's cold,
I take no care though he speaks me fair for the new
    love casts out the love that's old.

I take no care for the blessed prayer, for my mother's
    hand or my mother's call.
There ever rings in my ear, and sings, a voice more
    dear and more sweet than all.
Cold, cold's my breast, and broke's my rest, and
    O it's blest to be dead I'd be,
Held safe and fast from the fairy blast, and deaf at
    last to the Ceol-Sidhe !

A Marriage Charm

HERE and now, by the angel-orders nine,
That take no care for love nor yet for loss,
Woman most dear, I choose you out for mine,
I turn my errant feet your way across.

I set a charm upon your hurrying breath,
I set a charm upon your wandering feet,
You shall not leave me—not for life, nor death,
Not even though you cease to love me, Sweet.

A woman's love nine Angels cannot bind,
Nor any rune that wind or water knows,
My heart were all as well set on the wind,
Or bound, to live or die, upon a rose.

I set a charm upon you, foot and hand,
That you and Knowledge, love, may never meet,
That you may never chance to understand
How strong you are, how weak your lover, Sweet.

I set my charm upon your kindly arm,
I set it as a seal upon your breast ;
That you may never hear another's charm,
Nor guess another's gift outruns my best.

I bid your wandering footsteps me to follow,
Your thoughts to travel after in my track,
I am the sky that waits you, dear grey swallow,
No wind of mine shall ever blow you back.

I am your dream, Sweet : so no more of dreaming,
Your lips to mine must end this chanted charm,
Your heart to mine, 'neath nut-brown tresses stream-
    ing,
I set my love a seal upon your arm.

A Drowned Girl to Her Lover

I HEAR the hill-winds, I hear them calling
The long gray twilights and white morns thro',
The tides are rising, the tides are falling,
And how will I answer or come to you?
For over my head the waves are brawling
And I shall never come back to you!

Dark water's flowing my dark head over,
And where's the charm that shall bid it back?
Wild merrows sing, and strange fishes hover
Above my bed o' the pale sea-wrack:
And Achill sands have not kept for my lover
The fading print of my footstep's track.

Under the sea all my nights are lonely,
Wanting a song that I used to hear.
I dream and I wake and I listen only
For the sound of your footfall kind and dear,
Avourneen deelish, your Moirin's lonely
And is the day of our meeting near?

The hill-winds coming, the hill-winds going,
I send my voice on their wings to you, --
To you, ma bouchal, whose boat is blowing
Out where the green sea meets the blue:
Come down to me now, for there's no knowing
But the bed I lie in might yet hold two!

Meadow-Parsley

My Garland

I MAKE a garland here of water-flowers
    Gathered in quiet hours
From banks that Liris hourly eats away :
From fields that hear all day
The plaint of Simois for boyhood dead.
    From almond-boughs o'erhead
I pluck some mocking blossoms : and a spray
  Of euphrasy,
That I may see on every leafless tree
The promise of its later royalty
Of mellow apples, or its summer dower
    Of scarlet thorn or purple Judas-flower.
I make my garland here, and set between
    Pale poplar leaves and Pan's own parsley green
From battle-fields where Nike has not been.
I lift my finished wreath, but make my prayer
Neither to Jove nor Venus : nor have care
To plead to Juno, that my unbound hair
    The yellow veil may bear.
But I make humble prayer
To Pan, who gives the squirrel winter store,
Who bids the reeds grow by the river-shore :
    That he will stand before

My joy and grief,
And that my withered leaf
He gather up into his sunburned hand.
For joy and grief and hope Pan also knew,
And he hath care to-day for maid and man
That Love has yet forborne to bless or ban :
For once in fields that knew no mortal feet
He harvested Love's wheat, in Love's own land.
Therefore, my wreath that's pale and little sweet
I cast before Pan's feet.

Hymn to Pan

(To W. Beer)

Shall we not praise thee on the reed, the reed —
Shall we not praise thee who art lord indeed?
Lord of the bird and beast, of maid and man,
      The kindly Pan!

Lord of the flying hounds, the patient kine,
Lord of more kingdoms than our hearts divine:
Lord of each slender silver stream that ran
Among the reeds, the reeds that love thee, Pan!
Thy word makes bloom the purple columbine,
And shrivels up the grapes upon the vine,
   And swells the berries in the ivy-twine!
Thou art the lord of labour and of ease:
    The sturdy fir is thine,
And thistle-down that lifts upon the breeze.
Lord of the squirrels romping up the trees;
Lord of the Dryad-girls whose flutings fill
      The hollows of the hill:
And lord of Syrinx, lost but loving still.

Ah, Syrinx, Syrinx, how shouldst thou forget?
     A voice of vain regret
For ever stirs the reeds, the reeds that were
      No browner than thine hair!

They will not hush although the breathless air
Be dim with heat and emptied of all song;
    But always all day long
They sigh the weary race that Syrinx ran,
They sigh because thy chase is ended, Pan !

And why it is they sigh when no wind blows,
    There is one reed that knows.
One reed of all the reeds that sigh and sway
    All through the windless day :
One reed of all the reeds that bend and bow—
    One reed that holds the soul of Syrinx now.
Ah, now, if thou couldst chase, she would not flee,
    Now *she* desireth thee !
And if she followed once from thee that ran,
    Wouldst thou escape her, Pan ?

Thou art the lord of every fountain cool,
And Naiads know thee in the river pool,
    The secret wells and full :
Lord of the wayward Fauns that leap and play
Where dreamed the forest-Dryad yesterday :
(And lord to-morrow of a lonelier shade
Where no more Dryads, bold yet half afraid,
Laugh through the ruddy pine stems) sooth to say,
Lord art thou of To-morrow as To-day :
For though Time waxes old, and sad grows man,
Neither shall take thy kingship from thee, Pan.

Thou shalt be lord where beats the hasty blood,
Lord of the evil impulse and the good,
Lord of the crowded chambers of the brain,
Lord of the tares and lord of the good grain.

Thou shalt have part in wedding and in birth :
In thy name shall the dead go to the earth
And bless thee in their going : maid and man
Shall know thee near them in their love-time, Pan !

The green Earth gives thee praise,
For fruitful autumn days,
        For hawthorn-scented Mays,
For rainy Aprils : Junes that set ablaze
The world with roses : for the crowning boon
Of the broad harvest moon !

Also we praise thee for the stormy days,
For marsh-fires that we took for stars a space,
    For Hope's divine delays :
And for the rapture in the mother's face.

        For battles lost and won,
        For rise and set of sun
        For winds that ruffle up the waters gray,
        For ships that sail away :
For gifts with-held since Time his race began,
We praise thee, Pan !

The Faun to his Shadow

(W. B.)

The Faun said to his shadow, "How can I dance
    or play
When never an Oread beckons me at dawning of
    the day ?
When never an Oread, rosy-limbed, laughs through
    the living grass
Or leans adown the river-bank to make the stream
    her glass ?"

The Faun said to his shadow, " The days are over-
    long,
The very ousel-cock begins to pipe a sadder song
Oh, short sweet days of summer, would that I slept
    with you
In your nest lined warm with faded flowers, old
    kisses and lost dew !

Oh, faded flowers of fennel, that will not bloom
    again
For any south wind's calling, for any magic rain—

What gold is left in all the world, what gold for me
    to win ?
What shadows worth the hiding in, what sorrow
    worth the sin ?

And you, O dear dead Oreads, I would not have
    you back,
For the world's old, and the world's cold, and love
    is turned to lack.
Better for me to leave these fields forlorn, these
    meadows gray,
And follow your fading footsteps upon the sunless
    way—
And find—who knows what a Faun may find beyond
    the night and day ?"

A Song of Five

Two shepherds sat a-piping beneath the olives gray,
What times three Thracian maidens came singing
    up the way :
Two shepherds sat a-courting upon the windy lea,
But two the tale of shepherds : the shepherd-maids
    were three.

Oh, Daphnis sang of Lais, and idle Dion told
How blue were eyes of Thais, how locked her heart
    and cold :
And all the while the olives were sighing soft to see
That none might bring the grace to sing of white
    Autonoë.

There was no grace in any feast that Thais lacked
    for guest,
Her coming flushed the pallid East, her going dulled
    the West.
Oh, pale when Lais' cheek was nigh each wreathed
    and rosy shell,
And birds might put their piping by, sweet Lais sang
    so well.

Thais would go silk threads to sew upon a warrior's
 banner,
Lais would dwell a queen in hell with ghostly maids
 to fan her.
And Daphnis would fare fishing with nets upon the
 sea,
And each were fain some grace to gain save white
 Autonoë.

They saw the brown sails lifting, they heard the
 sailors cry,
And Dion dreamed of drifting past shores where
 mermaids lie :
And Daphnis took his idle flute, and blew so ten-
 derly,
That Thais slept, and Lais wept, and smiled
 Autonoë.

Now, out, alas ! that summers pass and music lasts
 not long ;
O'er Dion's bed grow lilies red, and bees make
 droning song :
The sea-waves cradle Lais, and only seaweeds see
If hair and lips of Thais still gold and scarlet be.

But Daphnis blows upon his flute by Hades' shadowy
 throne ;
And after him with hasty foot, Autonoë alone,
A living maid, has followed, who, if she would,
 could tell
How fair love makes the tangled brakes and fields
 forlorn of hell.

Phæacia

(To W. H. Chesson)

To the Phæacian Islands let us go,
　　Let us link hands and go—
And bid farewell to all the jealous Gods
In almond-flowers that muffle up their rods—
　　The Gods who give
Long life to such as have no heart to live:
And shed swift death upon beloved heads.
The Gods who give us amaranth and moly,
And plant our battle-fields with parsley-beds ;
The Gods who shame the proud and scorn the lowly.
　This also have they given
　A little space wherein dull earth turns heaven,
　But all the while Fate's wheel, beset with eyes,
　　Turns, breaking butterflies.
　　Let us rise up and go
To the Phæacian Islands where they lie
Gray, 'neath a grayer sky—
" At the light's limit," where the light is low,
　　And no winds blow.

For here the autumn air is sharp with dreams
　　Of snow to come,

And on leaf-muffled roads our feet fall dumb,
     By silent streams.
After the summer let us turn and go
     Beyond the deathly snow,
Beyond the breath of any winter wind—
The hands that hold us back are all unkind,
     (Ah, hands unkind
That fain would hold us when we fain would go
To dimmer, dearer lands than these we know,
Even as we know the faces of our kin—)
The gates of ivory that we would win
Stand open, and we fain would enter in :
To the light's limit where the light is low,
     Sweet, shall we go ?

And there nor summer burns, nor winter breathes
Death's message to the roses, withering :
But the Phæacians know perpetual spring,
Nor any tempest works their meadows wrong ;
     A year of April, always wavering
     'Twixt sun and rain,
No harvest hopes or fears the whole year long.
     But always these are theirs,
The doubtful pleasure that is half a pain,
The ghost of sorrow that is almost fain,
So old it is ; and Hope that turns again
     Before she takes farewell
Of fields that she has sown with wheat and tares—
     Here in this drowsy land
Joy is not known, and Grief takes Sleep by hand :
     And by the shadowy streams
White poppies nodding grow, fulfilled of dreams.
Here in green leaves her light the lily sheathes,
And here the rose is always in the bud,

Nor any silver brook is vexed with flood,
Or, thinned with drought, slips seaward through
    the dry
And sunburnt rushes all the long July.

Let us go hence and find those islands fair,
    Go hence, and take no care
For Lydian flutes that falter far away :
Let us go hence, and take no thought for all
The Linus-songs whose long lamentings fall
Like rain, like rain round our departing feet.
    These songs are over-sweet,
And we are weary of the homespun day,
And we are sick for shadows : let's away !
Link hands and let us go, ere we grow old.
    (Your hand is cold :)
Loose hands and let us go, ere we grow old,
To mistier meadows and a softer sky,
There in Phæacia let us live and die.
Nay : but not die, alas !   No mortal dies
Who eats of lotus 'neath Phæacian skies :
    Who finds life's tune too long
    May never break the song
Though to each note the sick heart rings untrue.
But there grow magic flowers wherewith to twine
A garland half divine :
    Eyebright and bitter rue,
    Weird mandragore and moly—
Hyacinth sweet as sin and lilies holy :
Pale iris growing where the streams wind slowly
Round the smooth shoulders of untrodden hills ;
White meadowsweet and yellow daffodils.
There shall we go, dear heart, our lives to crown ?
    For all our garlands here are late leaves brown,

And bitter rue :
There shall we go and lay our burdens down,
 And drink of youth anew ?
There shall we go where no one dreams of death,
 . . . Or love—or faith ?

There shall we go, or shall we rather stay
 Here, in the common day,
And watch Love's eyes grow dim, Love's head turn
  gray ?
We will let be those isles of gramarye,
 And magic flowers let be,
To pluck our earthly thyme and columbine :
And stay where love and death are mine and thine.

Shepherds' Song

" ALL alas and welladay,"
　　(Shepherds say)
Stepping with a stealthy pace
　　Past the place
Where the idle lilies blow !
" Here Diana dreaming lay
　　(Snow in snow !)
Lay a-dreaming on a day
　　Long ago."

Few the prayers the shepherds say
　　(Welladay !)
Now Diana ends her chase,
　　Giving place
To a maid with softer eyes,
　　Colder breast
(Mystery of mysteries !)
　　For her greatest gift, and best—
　　Giving rest.

" Now we thole," the shepherds say,
" Shorter night and longer day.
　　Shorter days
Sweeter were : when in the nights
Came a sudden press of lights :

Came the shining of a face
  Far away.
And we gave Diana praise
For the passing of her face.

" All alas and welladay ! "
    (Shepherds say)
" Maiden rule we still obey,
Yet we loved the first maid best.
    Terror-prest
Though we fled by herne and hollow,
Fearing angry shafts to follow,
Dead, we knew that we should rest
    On her breast."

" All alas and welladay,"
    (Shepherds say)
" Earth was green that now is gray :
Auster dared not any day
    Beat or blow,
When mid lilies Dian lay
    (Snow in snow !)
Lay a-dreaming on a day
    Long ago."

Helen of Troy

I am that Helen, that very Helen
Of Leda, born in the days of old :
Men's hearts were as inns that I might dwell in :
Houseless I wander to-night, and cold.

Because man loved me, no God takes pity :
My ghost goes wailing where I was Queen!
Alas ! my chamber in Troy's tall city,
My golden couches, my hangings green !

Wasted with fire are the halls they built me,
And sown with salt are the streets I trod,
Where flowers they scattered and spices spilt me—
Alas, that Zeus is a jealous God !

Softly I went on my sandals golden ;
Of love and pleasure I took my fill ;
With Paris' kisses my lids were holden,
Nor guessed I, when life went at my will,
That the Fates behind me went softlier still.

A Nymph's Lament

(To W. H. C.)

O, SISTER NYMPHS, how shall we dance or sing
    Remembering
What was and is not?   How sing any more
Now Aphrodite's rosy reign is o'er?
    For on the forest-floor
Our feet fall wearily the summer long,
    The whole year long:
No sudden Goddess through the rushes glides,
No eager God among the laurels hides;
Jove's eagle mopes beside an empty throne,
Persephone and Ades sit alone
    By Lethe's hollow shore.
    And hear not any more
Echoed from poplar-tree to poplar-tree,
The voice of Orpheus making sweetest moan
    For lost Eurydice.
The Fates walk all alone
In empty kingdoms, where is none to fear
Shaking of any spear.
Even the ghosts are gone
From lightless fields of mint and euphrasy:
There sings no wind in any willow-tree,

And shadowy flute-girls wander listlessly
Down to the shore where Charon's empty boat,
As shadowed swan doth float,
Rides all as listlessly, with none to steer.
A shrunken stream is Lethe's water wan
Unsought of any man :
Grass Ceres sowed by alien hands is mown,
And now she seeks Persephone alone.

The Gods have all gone up Olympus' hill,
And all the songs are still
Of grieving Dryads, left
To wail about our woodland ways, bereft,
The endless summertide.
Queen Venus draws aside
And passes, sighing, up Olympus' hill.
And silence holds her Cyprian bowers, and claims
Her flowers, and quenches all her altar-flames,
And strikes dumb in their throats
Her doves' complaining notes :
   And sorrow
Sits crowned upon her seat : nor any morrow
Hears the Loves laughing round her golden chair.
(Alas, thy golden seat, thine empty seat !)
Nor any evening sees beneath her feet
The daisy rosier flush, the maidenhair
And scentless crocus borrow
From rose and hyacinth their savour sweet.

Without thee is no sweetness in the morn,
The morn that was fulfilled of mystery,
It lies like a void shell, desiring thee,
O daughter of the water and the dawn,
   Anadyomene !

There is no gold upon the bearded corn,
No blossom on the thorn ;
And in wet brakes the Oreads hide, forlorn
Of every grace once theirs : no Faun will follow
    By herne or hollow
Their feet in the windy morn.

Let us all cry together " Cytherea ! "
Lock hands and cry together : it may be
That she will heed and hear
And come from the waste places of the sea,
Leaving old Proteus all discomforted,
To cast down from his head
Its crown of nameless jewels, to be hurled
In ruins, with the ruined royalty
Of an old world.
The Nereids seek thee in the salt sea-reaches,
Seek thee ; and seek, and seek, and never find :
Canst thou not hear their calling on the wind ?
We nymphs go wandering under pines and beeches,
And far—and far behind
We hear Pan's piping blown
After us, calling thee and making moan
(For all the leaves that have no strength to cry,
   The young leaves and the dry),
Desiring thee to bless these woods again,
    Making most heavy moan
    For withered myrtle-flowers,
    For all thy Paphian bowers
    Empty and sad beneath a setting sun ;
      For dear days done !

The Naiads splash in the blue forest-pools—
   " Idalia—Idalia ! " they cry.
     " On Ida's hill,

With flutings faint and shrill—
On Ida's hill the shepherds vainly try
Their songs, and coldly stand their damsels by,
    Whatever tunes they try ;
For beauty is not, and Love may not be,
      On land or sea—
Oh, not in earth or heaven, on land or sea,
While darkness holdeth thee."

The Naiads weep beside their forest-pools,
And from the oaks a hundred voices call,
"Come back to us, O thou desired of all !
Elsewhere the air is sultry : here it cools,
And full it is of pine-scents : here is still
The world-pain that has driven from Ida's hill
    Thine unreturning feet.
Alas ! the days so fleet that were, and sweet,
When kind thou wert, and dear,
And all the Loves dwelt here !
Alas ! thy giftless hands, thy wandering feet !
Oh, here for Pithys' sake the air is sweet,
And here snow falls not, neither burns the sun,
Nor any winds make moan for dear days done.
Come, then : the woods are emptied all of glee,
And all the world is sad, desiring thee !"

Castara's Flitting

(To L. Francis)

Bring roses for Castara's breast—
Nay, no more roses bring.
Let be the rose where she blooms best
Castara's followed Spring.

I know a path with poppies red,
Milk-white with blossomed May,
Linden and birch meet overhead:
And that's Castara's way.

O well befall thee, happy way—
Fair fall thy poppies red!
Be thy skies blue though ours are gray
And all our roses dead.

For, O our poppies all are white—
And life's a weary thing,
Since, taking from our eyes the light,
Castara's followed Spring.

Helen

(To W. B.)

FAIR star that shone on Sparta, torch of Troy,
Thy sorrow on our lips is turned to joy—
     So sweet it is to-day—
The burden of a beauty passed away
Into the shadowy isles beyond the West:
The burden of old griefs that vexed thy breast,
     The tale of loves that stay,
Kind loves, and old, that yet make sweet delay,
     (Ah, Helen, Helen!)
We also knew thee in our golden years,
     (Ah, Helen, Helen!)
We cried thy name above the shattering spears,
     Music in all men's ears:
 A light, a light down all the darkening years.
We saw thee looking from the leaguered wall:
We heard the feet of Gods pass wistfully
     From Priam's hall
What time the city darkened to its fall.
We looked on Helen, and went out to die.
     (Ah, Helen, Helen!)

We died, and took thy praises to the throne
    Of dark Persephone
('The throne built fair of jade and ebony),
And every wailing wind abroad has blown
    The glory of thy face.
  Even the echoes of this shadowy place
    Have one sweet word to say—
      (Ah, Helen, Helen!)
      And still thy fame flits on
  Repeated by the poplars still that sway
  With sighs for ill deeds wrought, for good undone.
And out beyond the marsh of Acheron.
We sought all day for what poor blossoms grow
    Along the windy lea,
And yellow poppies found that love the sea,
Great poppies red and poppies white of blee—
Then shod with silence, pale as shadows are,
Then to thy dreams we came, past bolt and bar:
And laid our heavy poppies all a-row
    Beside thy bed—
And laid our futile kisses, soft as snow,
    Upon thy golden head.
    (Ah, Helen, Helen!)

Yea: and we stole great lilies red as blood
From sleeping brows of ghostly maids that stood
(Like poplars gathered round a cypress-tree),
    That all day served and stood
Around the throne of dark Persephone.
And these we brought in morning dreams to thee.
    (Ah, Helen, Helen!)
We brought thee gifts of flags and bearded corn
    From out the fields forlorn,
Where strong with walls and gateways faced with gold

                      H

Troy stood of old.
We brought thee yellow roses for the sorrow
 That met thee every morrow :
We brought thee maiden lilies full of dew
From ruined gardens that thy soft feet knew
 When we were sons of Tyre,
And thou requitedst us with gifts of fire,
  (Ah, Helen, Helen !)

And last : we came to thee with footsteps slow,
  (Ah, Helen, Helen !)
And laid strange flowers where thou wert lying low,
 Strange flowers, as cold as snow—
More softly red than lips we used to know,
  (Ah, Helen, Helen !)
Flowers that were gathered up by alien hands,
 In those wild meadow lands
  Where the pale Parcæ pause
To watch their snowy poppies how they grow.
Pond-lilies in whose cups the shining was
 Half water and half flame :
Flowers of old love, old grief, and older shame,
 Strange flowers without a name.
Diana's lilies, dead but still divine—
Field-flowers of Enna, dropped by Proserpine :
Myrtles from Cyprus gardens : olive-boughs
 Warm from Athene's brows—
All these we brought to Helen where she lay,
 Blind to the calling day—
  (Ah, Helen, Helen !)

We crowned her one by one, then left her there
 With deathless garlands on her golden hair,
  And took our silent way

Across that lake where never sunlight lay
    Whose waves are sullen flame :
  And never one of all that company
  Bound for the dim halls of Persephone—
Greek, Trojan, Tyrian but at heart was glad,
Nor thought he once on grief he might have had.
For with us, fairer far than words may say,
    The ghost of Helen came.
And we, who loved her, we were glad that day,
    (Ah, Helen, Helen !)

April Desiring Aphrodite

(To Elsa D'Esterre-Keeling)

Long days has April wept December's death,
And now the folded ferns await thy breath,
Mother : and not a lark its service saith.

Whether thou dwellest in the hollow seas,
Or where the shepherds pipe upon the leas
Of Arcady, beneath the apple-trees,

We know not, Mother : who are we to know ?
But we have seen the snowdrops in the snow,
And fain would see again the lilac blow.

Rise up: and leave the myrtle groves forlorn :
Shut fast the Ivory Doors, the Gate of Horn
Set wide, and let the faithful dreams be borne

To all the grievéd sleepers : late indeed
Thou comest to put life in soil and seed,
Yet come to us who of thy life have need.

What of the night gone by and overpast ?
The winter of our discontent at last
Goes driving by like sleet upon the blast.

On some black bough an ousel tries his note,
And a far lark sends from his golden throat
A cry of joy, most tender and remote.

A crocus on my lawn prinks out in gold.
And green leaves peep, half shrinking from the cold,
Where roses were and lilies grew of old.

Come : for the eggs are quickening in the nest,
And love is kindling in the maiden breast :
Come : we will give thee of our loveliest.

We will give milk and doves and honey-wine,
And folded buds of may and columbine :
Come, Aphrodite, to this world of thine !

Hebe

LET none now sing of Hebe : let none sing,
For she has said farewell to sun and spring :
Her feet on alien paths are wandering
Not known of Jove, and to the Dawn not dear.
Her lips remember not their former cheer,
Her cheeks forget the roses that they wore,
Her hands to cups of gold are set no more :
But she bends down by Lethe's sedgy bank,
And drinks the bitter waters Cora drank ;
And eats, unscathed, the apples that of old
Helen of Argos bought, with steel for gold.

Let none now sing of Hebe : songs are still
With her, and sighing : since death's hands fulfil
Life's broken promises.   She, being dead,
Has drawn the veil of Isis, and has read
The runes of the All-Father, in low lands
Sun burns not nor moon whitens: where the brands
Of sunrise and of sunset dare not flame
Nor thunder wakens at the Thunderer's name.
She has touched life and death, and goeth clad
In wisdom such as never Hermes had :
Let none now weep for Hebe, she being glad.

January

I am a mighty Hunter, I : a Hunter before the
    Lord ;
The lean white bears they know me, and come and
    go at word :
The Northern Lights are my dancing girls, the
    Hunter Star's my mate,
And we talk o'nights of Diana dead, and the Gaul-
    folk at the gate.

(Oh golden head of Diana dead, if I came on your
    sleep one day,
And one—no more—of the secret store of your
    kisses locked away,
If I should kneel from your lips to steal, you of the
    olive bough,
Oh blue eyes cold under brows of gold, would your
    anger smite me now ?

Oh sweet and stern, would you only turn, sighing,
    amid your sleep,
And dream again of some battle-plain and fire on
    some towered keep.
And never dream you were kissed of him who must
    walk in the endless snow.
Nor any rest- -such as keeps your breast —till the
    Judgment Day may know?

Oh stern and sweet, if I kissed your feet, would
you wake and listen and hear,
And turn your life from the endless strife of sword
and axe and spear ?
But 'tis best to sleep since the night is deep on
Egypt and Greece and Rome,
And the dust is shed upon Hera's head and Venus
has passed in foam).

And we talk o'nights of our outland fights, and of
kingdoms won and lost,
Our skates they ring on the ice and sing of the
frozen fjords we've crossed.
And a rose I have that no summer gave and the
sunset's rose is fair—
But though no rose rest on Orion's breast, he has
held a Pleiad there.

My servant, Wind, ere Fate did find herself too
old to play,
All unafraid 'twixt sun and shade, kissed half her
gloom away.
And gardens green he hath entered in, but counsel
close keeps he,
And what he knows of the rose, the rose, he will
not sing to me.

You have sung, God wot, of a hunter's lot, of bears
in the ice-caves green,
Of silent lips, and of goodly ships that are not, but
have been :
You have made a song of my north wind strong, of
the track of my feet in the snow :
But of strife that's mine, and of life that's mine,
what word do ye rhymers know ?

Ye ha' painted me with a face before, and a face
    that looketh back,
But I go as a man goes out to war, and I turn not
    on my back :
Nay, not for the stars in Orion's belt, or the stars
    in his long blade's sweep ;
A changeless place, 'twixt the snow and the stars
    for the Master of Stars I keep !

Arrow Song

THE land is alight with the sword and the arrow,
The light, long arrow, the fire of the bow—
The need-fires blaze upon hill and barrow
And fire and fuming as sisters go.
From open sea to the fjord that's narrow,
The longships dart through the rain of stones—
A bowman loosens his shining arrow,
It leaps to its mark - and a woman moans.

As fire through the forest sweeps the Viking,
As fire's the flight of his long, light dart :
As molten fire is the sunlight, striking
On the golden harness that shields his heart.
With fire and flaming from breast to barrow,
From dusk to darkness the Vikings go :
As Thor's own bolt is the flying arrow,
The light, long arrow, the fire of the bow.

Heimdal

In the old days there went amid forlorn
Ways o' the world, Heimdal the Wanderer:
Ways loved of all wild things of plume and fur.
Now Heimdal stands aloof, and wild things mourn.
He hears the long grass growing and he knows
The dropping silence of the polar snows:
Nor from his memory is one bird's cry lost.
Nine worlds are dreams within his dreaming eyes,
May-flies are born and die upon his hand
That helped to paint the sea-weeds and the skies,
And rosemary grows where he takes his stand.
O thou that countest leaf and flower and flake,
Touch our hearts lightly, lightly lest they break.

Ballad of the Linden

THE Linden in Upsala grows so well,
Of the linden-tree is a tale to tell.

There nested a dove in the linden-tree,
As fair as ever a bird may be.

She moaned and murmured the livelong day
For her own true mate that had flown away.

She moaned and mourned and no rest took she,
For the gray wings gone from the linden-tree.

The Princess came from her bower high,
"It's O," said she, "for good leave to die.

It's O for my heart and the round red sun,
Asleep together and grieving done!

There's a desolate dove in the tree-top here,
Like me would die and go seek her dear :

But her nest she has and her fledglings three,
And where is the nest for my babe and me?"

Where the Silver Spears keep the kind green land,
Earl Gerald kisses his young bride's hand :

All hung with white is the bride-chamber,
And the bride's tall brothers are lighting her ;

All hung with green is the linden-bough,
And stars are lamps for the Princess now.

She lies her lone, and in sorrow dumb
She prays that the dawn may never come.

Shall a ghost's eyes help her her weird to dree !
The ghost of a live man, oversea ?

The sin was of twain but there bides but one
To wind the tangle the Norns have spun ;

(And soft and silken is golden hair
To kiss when one wakes in the bride-chamber.)

O dark head, low 'neath the linden-tree,
Thank God, thank God that no eyes can see —

Though rain fall fast on the linden-bough,
Thank God that love is far from thee now !

That love has other kind eyes to read,
And rest thee still, for thy weird is dree'd.

Against the wind that to dawn grows cold,
She laps her babe in her mantle's gold.

She wraps him close that no eyes may see,
And Death and Morning her gossips be.

The dove croons low that no least leaf hears
What the mother breathes in her gossips' ears.

And dry are the gray eyes that weeping were,
So well her gossips do comfort her.

The green land's glad of the morning-tide,
And Gerald wakens by Gunhild's side :

And thinks not once of a fairer may
Left shamed and sorry in Norroway.

Since sorrow ends in a little while,
Spend Gudrun's sorrow for Gunhild's smile :

For sorrow goes and the smile will stay,
And the miles are many to Norroway.

Voices are merry in bower and hall,
And into the sunshine the bride they call ;

They call her out to the golden years,
From her maiden hopes and her maiden fears.

Voices are calling in bower and bawn,
And Gudrun's name is wild in the dawn.

White wings and brown hair by wee gold head,
Mother and baby and dove lie dead.
    (And sleep in the night is sweet.)

The Glittering Plain

(To William Morris : Maker)

Far, far away the Glittering Plain
Lies over leagues of land and sea :
The bow stands fair against the rain,
And yet we cannot find the key
Whereby at last we might attain
Where Castle Heart's Delight may be.

Land of the living, far away
Your fields stand golden in the sun :
The King smiles and the Folk are gay
For youth renewed and sorrow done :
And reapers gather in the hay
Singing forth for joy of harvest won.

Hallblithe, alas ! moves not along
The ways : nor Hostage o' the Rose :
But hark, Erato leads the song
And Love himself with laughter goes
Midmost the maidens there that throng
To pull the hawthorn whence it grows.

Yet call us, call us once again,
Land of the Living ! sweet and strong
Thy spell lies on us, heart and brain,
Though in the night we grope, and long
Must seek, or ere our eyes are fain
Of flowers and fields no winters wrong.

At Sticklestead

Then hawks came flying from Harold's Island
And the mound-bees gathered, and stung them sore ;
And a ness of swords in the drift of Odin
Gleamed white a moment, then gleamed no more.

War-leeks were white in the gold sun-rising,
War-leeks are red now the sun goes down,
And Valkyrs gather in Valhall gateways,
And wives are watching in Oslö town.

Few hawks flew homewards to Harold's Island
And the hives of the mound-bees empty stand,
Eagles shriek over the drift of Odin,
And gray wolves come in a ghostly band.

War-leeks were white in the clear sun-rising,
War-leeks are red, now the sun goes down :
Valkyrs and Vikings are glad in Valhall,
And wives are wailing in Oslö town.

Ingeborg the Fair

" Hoist up, hoist up your silken sails
And flee in teeth of outland gales :
Better be dead and past all care
Than look on Ingeborg the Fair.

" Hoist up, hoist up your silken sails,
Stop ears against her nightingales :
The seagull's song to Norseman's ear
Rings far more sweet and far more dear.

" Hoist up, hoist up your sails of gray,
And turn the Serpent's head away.
Vikings, be deaf and dumb and blind,
And leave white Ingeborg behind."

But folded hangs the silken sail,
And weary grows the northland gale :
Captain and crew and minstrel all
Sit careless in the golden hall.

Tho' loud the north wind calls, and long
The burden of the minstrel's song—
Burden of wives and maids that wait
Their Vikings by the water's gate.

" Hoist up, hoist up your silken sails,
Flee in the teeth of outland gales :
Better be dead and past all care
Than look on Ingeborg the Fair."

Thor Asleep

(To William Morris)

Lord of the Plains of Trembling, Master of Bonds-
　　men—Thor,
Where are you sleeping, son of Earth, while the
　　men go down to the war ?
Are the Giants slain and the Giants' Bane laid by,
　　with its battles o'er ?

Do you sit by Sif and listen, O Thor the Thun-
　　derer,
While she tunes her harp to a drowsy rhyme of
　　woes and wars that were ?
Are the swords and slings forgotten things for love
　　of the songs of her ?

Yet she is a God's own daughter, and the wild
　　blood's in her, too—
She has watched the young lives spilling, and
　　trodden them down like dew :
Does she not long for the seagull's song, and the
　　ships in the midsea blue ?

Awake, O Sif, arise, O Sif, and bid thy lord up-
stand,
Draw close the belt about him, set Miölnir in his
hand—
Bid him rise and smite for Odin's right and the
sake of Odin's land.

For over the sleep of Bragi the fearless wild bees
hum,
And Frigga listens at her loom for steps that never
come :
And an ended story is Odin's glory, and the mouth
of Mimir's dumb.

Up, Thor, for Odin's honour : up, Sif, for the
Thunderer's !
Tho' Sigurd sleep at Brynhild's side, let sleep be
his and hers !
Open tho' late is Valhall gate, and the sleeping
fire it stirs.

Sing, Sif, till the heroes hear thee—and rise, and
northward go
Till the Warder wakes on Bifrost bridge and
Balder wakes below ;
Till the Warder wakes and the sunrise breaks
the frozen heart of the snow.

Sing, Sif, till the ears of Odin hear thee, until Hel's
door
Be opened wide for Balder, and Frigga's watch be
o'er—
Sing, Gold-Hair, sing until Glasir ring with the
steps of Tyr and Thor.

The Gods of Egypt

(To W. B.)

A SONG to you, you vanished Gods of Khem,
Made by a dweller in the tents of Shem,
And pray you hear me sing a little while
Your mysteries withdrawn from banks of Nile
That feel your scarabs basking in the sun,
And hear your legends when the day is done.
Lord Amen, in the dusk that dost abide
Wilt thou not come forth, hearing lightly cried
Thy name that none dare speak in those dim days
Before the birth of minstrels that made praise
To lilies woven in Taia's dusky hair—
And roses that Rhodope's cheek made fair?
But since the gloom that on thine eyelids lies
Holds women very fair and very wise,
Rhodope, Cleopatra, Nitocris—
Is there for thee in darkness any bliss
That there thou walkest with unhastening feet
After the sunlight finding shadows sweet?

Of old was Khem a Lily, white and gold,
A slim Papyrus, goodly to behold:
But now the Lily lifts a dying face,
And withered is Papyrus in her place.

Lady of reeds and lilies, now she stands,
With wistful blinded eyes, and groping hands ;
Magicians cannot help her with their dreams,
Rust eats the uræus-crown, and Egypt seems—
The flood upon her, and no friendly ark—
A drowned maid drifting in the outer dark.
No help remains in alien Gods she knew :
No help in the strong Gods of Eridhu.
There is no comfort more in any star :
The Lily and Papyrus faded are.

Each sunset vests dark Khem in gold and red,
Yet Phrah and all the Pharaohs' fame is shed :
Each sunrise hangs an opal on the brow
Of the dumb Sphinx : but where is Sekhet now ?
What word of all his wisdom speaketh Seb ?
Neith sits and slumbers o'er her finished web ;
Nor cares she that from ringing shore to shore,
Her builders' chisels give her praise no more :
Nor that across her knees the lizards creep,
Her wheel is still, and very sound her sleep.
Anubis drowses by Amenti's gate,
Thoth and his ibis keep a lonely state,
Somewhere where lotus-lilies idly blow,
And Selk amid her scorpions lieth low.

Guinevere

(To Ellen Terry)

Amid the blossoms of the whitethorn wood,
Flower of all flowers, in Arthur's dream she stood,
No lily, but a rose of womanhood.

Gold veil blown backward from her golden hair,
Green-clad like young leaves in the April air:
Too fair the dream is, Arthur: deadly fair !

Yet thou shalt have the rose awhile to hold,
But for its sweetness' sake thy hearth grows cold—
Thy sword is rusted all for hair of gold !

How should he dream of sorrow, shame, or fear,
So loud the birds sang round the magic mere
Whose lightest ripple whispered "Guinevere !"

How should he dream of grief who dreams of love ?
Or guess how sore the cage shall fret his dove
When she grows weary of the gold thereof ?

Dream : it is good to dream when day is young—
Thy Queen shall dream another wood among
When love has loosed the bonds on Lancelot's
tongue.

Dream : as in Avalon (if oaths hold good)
To-day thou dreamest of her as she stood
Among the blossoms of the whitethorn wood.

Dream : I, too, dream who saw but yesterday
Queen Guinevere among the blossomed may,
A rose, a rose that shall not fade away.

Not fade, nor fail, but quicken still men's blood
In an uncourtly age, a lighter mood —
A rose that blossoms in a whitethorn wood.

Columbines

Sing a song of columbines
    (Doves within a nest),
Fairer nosegay no lad twines
    For his Chloe's breast—
Purple all for lover's pain,
    White for loyalty,
Take your roses, bring again
    Columbines for me.

Sing a song of columbines,
    White and purple-stoled,
Ere the bloom is on the bines,
    When the nights are cold—
They will watch the roses out,
    (Rose though Chloe be—
What care I if Chloe flout?)
    Columbines for me.

Apples

"Burden of rosy apples here I bear ;
Apples as sweet as sin, and half as fair :
Draw near, and eat, as Eve ate once, of old -
And gather wisdom ere you gather gold.
Ah, why delay ?   Look deep into my eyes –
Am I not beautiful ?   Am I not wise -
Though I too once walked free in Paradise ?
Most fair I am, although my eyes are cold :
Draw near, and win the apples that I hold.
The apples half I give and half deny :
Lo, I am Lilith ! will ye eat and die ? "

"Am *I* a stranger that ye stand so far-- ?
My foes that were, my kinsmen now that are
My foes that were, my lovers that shall be
By grace of kindly blood poured out for ye.
Am I a stranger ? yet my fruit's as red
As hers, that tempts the quick to be the dead.
You welcomed her a barren while ago
And me with stoning, even as a foe
You turned away from paths your footsteps know.
Now she hath cast you out, and here ye see
Come back to seek your grace, my fruit and me.
Ye know me now a little, yet God wot,
Indeed I loved ye while ye knew me not.
Lo ! here I stand to-day with fruit to give,
Azrael and his apples : eat and live !"

Outward Bound

I WILL go down to the calling sea,
Take ship for the Fortunate Isles, and sail
To lowlands dim where the poplars pale
Sigh long, sigh low for Persephone,
Where long she waits on the yellow strand
Demeter's voice and Demeter's hand.

I will go down to the calling sea,
Take ship for the Fortunate Isles, and find
The golden West, where the sirens bind
Their hair with garlands of briony,
Where time's forgot and no head grows gray,
And a wind blows merrily night and day.

I will go down to the calling sea,
Take ship for the Fortunate Isles, and follow
The wayward gull and the wind-blown swallow
Wherever the will of the wind may be :
And sweet sea-voices I'll surely hear
Though the Fortunate Isles come never near.

I will go down to the calling sea,
Though never a pilot may with me go :
With all sails set though I surely know
That wreck is waiting my ship and me—
And death the light at my mast-head shown,
For water and wind I have made my own.

Lament

FOR

EARL PATRICK STEWART

O THE leaves are turning brown towards October,
The Peerie Summer's well on the wane ;
And it's O I wad my life were also waning
Like a tide that kens no flood again.

And wild the gulls are crying round the nesses,
And wild the gulls cry far out at sea ;
But wilder cries the bird that's in my bosom—
" Earl Patrick, will ye no come back to me ?"

What care I for the auld wives' tale of treason ?
For the Heading-hill, O what care I ?
Dead or living, here's my welcome to Earl Patrick,
And a kind arm where his head may lie.

Put by the matted grasses and the charlocks,
And your dreams put off, and let them be :
One hour steal frae the Deil, Earl Patrick,
And, O dear heart, come back to me !

La Belle Dame Sans Mercy

(To Edwin Oliver)

East o' the Sun, West o' the Moon
They all must go who'd find her boon.
    (La Belle Dame Sans Mercy !)

West o' the Moon, East o' the Sun,
Thither are many roads that run,
But the right road is the only one.
    (La Belle Dame Sans Mercy !)

Her heart (woe's me !) is locked and cold
A secret chamber filled with gold.
    (La Belle Dame Sans Mercy !)

Straight as a lily-wand is she,
Her face is pale as lilies be,
Her brown hair floweth to her knee.
    (La Belle Dame Sans Mercy !)

Her hands are idle hands and white,
They spin nor weave by day or night.
    (La Belle Dame Sans Mercy !)

And yet those slender hands, God wot,
Have dug graves in her garden plot
'Neath tangles of forget-me-not.
    (La Belle Dame Sans Mercy!)

There is no Saint in Paradise
Bends brows above such holy eyes.
    (La Belle Dame Sans Mercy!)

And be her eyes or blue or grey,
There lives no man on earth to say,
Yet her eyes draw men's souls away
    (La Belle Dame Sans Mercy!)

And who dare kiss her on the mouth
Knows no more hunger, no more drouth.
    (La Belle Dame Sans Mercy!)

And whoso she hath kissed again
Is blest among all other men :
But Heaven's gate shuts him agen
And La Belle Dame Sans Mercy.

Frauenlob

Lover of Ladies, 'tis not long
    (Not long as loving goes)
Since you were known of laugh and song,
    Of rue and rose.
But now your hot heart cools to dust,
    Forgot of game and glee,
As heavy hearts and light hearts must,
    With rosemary.
For all your garlands dipt in wine —
    (Rose-garlands oversweet)
Now ivy-tendrils clasp and twine
    At head and feet.
Dream now of Gabriel's golden wings,
    Of Michael sweet and strong :
Of wet brakes whence a mavis sings
    All the day long.
Dream thus until your wings shall grow,
    And purged of earthly leaven—
Lover of Ladies, you shall go
    Mid fields of heaven.

To the Ladies Des Baux

(To W. B.)

LADIES of Arles and of Les Baux,
Where do your roses bloom to-day ?
Such roses as no gardens grow
Since the world put off green for gray.
Ah ! gay Baussette and Étiennette,
Have yours, too, fallen dim and dead,
Or are they warm and fragrant yet,
Your heavy roses, dusky-red ?

Where are the songs that Cabestan
Made long ago to your gold hair,
Your eyes' gray fire that shamed the dawn,
Your mouth's red blossom, Berengère ?
And Château-Vert's forgot, Berard,
The châtelaine's forgotten, too,—
And Marie dwells where shadows are
And keeps, may be, no thought of you.

Passe-Rose has passed all roses by,
Except Death's roses white of blee :
And none of all her lovers sigh
That France grows no such flower as she !
So for a little time, farewell,
You roses of a warmer day,
Till I come also where you dwell,
Where Love is blind and needs must stay.

St. Maurice

I SLEPT and entered in " the blissful place
Of the heart's heal, and deadly woundës' cure,"
Where Love is wingless found, and Faith is sure,
And men and maidens look in God His face.
There, where green leaves twine closely in a bower,
St. Maurice and his Theban men mount guard,
And on each breast I saw the martyr's sard
Burn in the white cup of a lily-flower.
O bold St. Maurice, is it good to rest
Here amid asphodels and lilies sown ?
Or do you sometimes wish the old time back,
When you were tried with sword and fire and wrack,
Yet kept unhurt the bird within your breast,
Whose voice with peace has somewhat tuneless
    grown ?

Lily and Lad's Love

Oh Irish lily, tall and white,
Among green tangled southernwood,
Your folded flower of maidenhood
Folds closer up from touches light
Of idle fingers.   Sweet, the night
Is coming when no work is good :
Will you stand aye in alien mood
Here at the edges of the fight ?

Oh, good to bloom here in your wood,
You shall live longer being unworn
On some man's breast : but life's forlorn
When life is lonely : winds are rude,
But some rough wind might change to sweet
Among the lad's love at your feet.

Red Rose

(To My Mother)

The Lily sweetens for no living lover,
But listens for the loitering feet of Death:
The Iris has strange secrets to discover,
Rosemary some old grief remembereth.
Forget-me-not's blue eyes are dim with passion,
Sir Humble-Bee has jilted Columbine,
Lavender's an old maid, and out of fashion,
And Madam Tulip's gown is over fine.

Red Rose alone is royal in her giving,
And is no niggard, all her gold being spent:
She gives her colour and her fragrance living,
And, being dead and dust, she gives her scent.
Red Rose, throned safe beyond all fear of treason,
Blenching no whit when rude hands shake your tree,
In season, noble Rose, and out of season—
In life, in dreams, in death, be friends with me!

Love-in-a-Mist

(To L. Norfolk)

Love-in-a-mist in every garden grows
Beside the hollyhock, beneath the rose :
Love-in-a-mist makes every rose less gay,
And takes the lily's gold and leaves her gray,
And turns the poppy pale as winter snows.
Sir Humble-bee will none of it, but goes
Straight for the sunflower in the garden-close,
And spiders' webs of silver will not stay
      Love-in-a-mist.
Who garners it we wist not, nor who sows,
Nor to what end its misty blossom blows :
Only its blue eyes meet us, day by day,
Till half we wish the mists would blow away.
Who knows true Love be sure he also knows
      Love-in-a-mist.

Octaves of the Wind

SURE, I was born mid blowing of a wind!
For when wild Euros spreads his pinions white
No bonds of flesh and blood my soul can bind
From sweeping forth with him into the night.
I know the wind's wild kisses: how they give
Strength to the soul they touch, to die or live:
And when the Norns my life's full skein have twined,
I shall go forth mid blowing of a wind.

There is like thee no prophet, rugged East!
Thy runes they are on solemn Stonehenge writ
Until the sun is dark, and Time has ceased,
Not to be understanded of man's wit.
I love thee, East, who shall love better none:
Of thy few worshippers, behold me one!
Meanwhile thy rough caresses make me brave
Against the day thou blowest o'er my grave.

There is like thee no victor, Viking East!
Beside thine, Merlin's is no mighty name:
Thou blowest—where is Agamemnon's fame,
Where Dian's priestess and Apollo's priest?
Thou hast laid all Dodona's oak-trees low,
O'er Stonehenge, unafraid, the swallows go—
On Aztec shrines thy wings have quenched the fire:
Because of thee the merchants weep for Tyre.

The burden of dead ladies was the word
The East wind vexed my dreams with yesterday :
How Mahild's hair was coloured like ripe hay,
And Aly's voice the sweetest ever heard—
How lightly fell the feet of Berengère,
How such a one was kind, and such was fair,
And how the Dance of Death called friend and foe ;
And now they must be sought with last year's snow.

Rose of Roses

(An Armenian Song)

Oh you were red and sweet as any rose,
Your branch reached higher than the lily grows,
Taller than fox-gloves in the garden-close---
     Ah, rose of roses,
     Raïssa, rose of roses !

You would not bloom for the delaying Spring,
Nor heed the sound of Autumn's minstreling.
Your love and life were swift as swallow's wing,
     Ah, rose of roses,
     Raïssa, rose of roses !

Of roses white they made your bridal bed,
On yellow roses lay your dying head,
Your grave is covered in with roses red :
     Ah, rose of roses !
     Raïssa, rose of roses !

Hathor

I sit beneath my fig-tree, while my kine
Pasture around me drowsily, knee-deep
In lilies, chewing sweetest cud of sleep,
While I sing softly to this wheel of mine.
A skein of many-coloured threads I twine
And know not why : nor why indeed I sing
Low, as the bees do in their wandering
From lotus unto lotus round my shrine.
My light is only sunset's : it burns low
And lower yet these seasons till I dread
The darkness creeping on me from the skies.
I loved the full fair nights of long ago
When Sphinx and Sekhet worked their mysteries !
Then I rocked Horus : now I rock the dead.

The Song of Jeanne de France

How slow, how slow the minutes pass,
What time I gaze across the leas,
And watch the dew dry off the grass,
    Heigho, Denise !

Spring walks abroad in green and gold,
And flushes all the almond-trees,
But still my heart is dark, and cold
    As death, Denise !

My father rules a kingdom fair,
My mother smiles in silken ease :
I go in velvet and in vair
    All day, Denise !

In velvet and in vair I go,
But children never clasp my knees,
And no kind lips my pale lips know,
    Heigho, Denise !

Some day, some day I'll surely hear
My name cried down the listening breeze,
And hear a voice more lief and dear
    Than yours, Denise !

And, hearing, I shall rise and go
Out from my prison, if God please :
Like cottage-girls, more glad, more low
     Than I, Denise !

Oh surely I shall quit my throne
To meet my lover on the leas,
And if the name whereby he's known
Be Death—why, *you* may then make moan,
     Not I, Denise !

A Song of the Road

(To My Mother)

All the mills in the world are grinding gold grain,
All hearts in the world like my heart should be fain
For my foot goes in time to a holiday measure
And the bird in my bosom is singing for pleasure.

Tall soldiers in gold stand the plumed ranks of corn,
And the poppies are dancing for joy of the morn :
They're gipsies and vagrants, the home-keepers say,
But my heart is at one with the poppies to-day.

I know not what end to my travel shall be,
Or what fairy Prince rides a-seeking for me—
He may be a Sheogue in graithing of gold,
Or a graybeard who tarries for young maids and old.

Meanwhile I go tramping the merry world over,
With the flower of my heart folded close for my
    lover :
Folded safely and close till my Prince come and
    claim
The bud long asleep, and the flower turn a flame.

Meanwhile I go tramping, a masterless maid,
With flowers blowing for me in sunshine and shade,
White poppies, red poppies, sea-poppies of amber,
And a wreath for my head of all wild vines that
 clamber.

I am one with the wind and the flowers in the corn,
And I and the wind laugh aloud in our scorn
At the bedesmen who quarrel earth's meadow-lands
 over,
While there's roses on bushes and honey in clover.

Osiris

(To William Beer)

O judge us kindly, Thou that judgest rightly
   All things that mortal are—
Men that lift up weak hands unto Thee nightly
   And every wandering star.
Thy sisters are the End and the Beginning,
   Thine is the empty hearth :
Thine, too, the quiet sleep for all men's winning
   In kindly earth :
And Thine, the souls that wake from sleep to
      sinning,
         Osiris.

We saw Thee not, Lord, in the crowded city,
   Nor in the market-place
Heard we the falling of Thy feet : have pity,
   Let Thy queen's hidden face
Be softened with Thy mercy at our crying ;
   Thy hand that slew painted the lotus-blossom,
   And sowed love's seed in the kind mother's bosom :
By Philæ, where Thy mortal part is lying,
We know ye live, we know that we are dying,
         Osiris !

Thou knowest we are weak : that we are strong
    We know not : for like waves
We fall and shatter, and a bridal song
    Breaks music round our graves.
We are the strings that help thy harp to sweetness.
    Alas ! we only sing
Sweet things borne down, and ruin that ends com-
      pleteness,
    Lord, and our King!
Thine is the dream, and Thine the dawn that
    breaks it ;
    We can but dream and die.
Thou art the song and the silence that o'ertakes it
    Ere yet the tears be dry.
Beside the labouring kine the neatherd trudgeth,
    At noon thou mak'st red earth of him again :
We cry against thee, "Who art thou that judgeth,
    Maker who marrest men ? "

Sighing Song

East o' the Sun, West o' the Moon,
  West o' the Moon, and far away,
  Beyond the night, beyond the day
There lies a country fair to see,
With apple-orchards green and boon.
Some day we'll travel there, maybe,
  Ere heads grow gray, and lamps burn low
    Heigho, heigho!

East o' the Sun, West o' the Moon,
  East o' the Sun, and far away,
The time is always afternoon,
  The month is always early May.
And ships we never thought to see
  Ride lightly in the bays below,
Green groves of elm and willow tree,
    Heigho, heigho!

East o' the Sun, West o' the Moon,
  For happy hearts who enter there,
No discord spoils the idlest tune
  Nor gray steals into golden hair;
Nor any lily fears the snow.
  Unending noon, unending May—
Yet Love is shy of entering there,
And dwells where life is not so fair,
Far, very far, and far away—
    Heigho, heigho!

L

A Winter Song

WHEN the Winter Way is white in the sky,
And the Vikings ha' laid their war-shields by,
Then I sit by the barrow and make my moan
That I walk alone and I sleep alone
    Since sleep holds Thorarin fast.

When the Winter Way shakes its silver snow
On the groaning pines and the graves below,
My heart is more cold than the Winter Way,
And under the gold hair my thoughts are gray,
    Since sleep holds Thorarin fast.

Lament for Leontium

ALAS! her lips were red:
But roses blush instead.

Her brows wore nobler white
Than lilies do, to-night.

Alas, what shall one say,
Save that her eyes were gray
Even as our skies to-day,
    Ai, ai, Leontium!

And for her yellow hair
Tall mullein blossoms there:

And for her laughter clear
The sea-wave shatters here.

Down ways her feet have known
Ways with weeds overgrown—
Only the dust is blown—
    Ai, ai, Leontium!

Finnish Bride-Song

BOUGHS of myrtle here I bring :
  Folds of pall and vair,
Silver cord and silken string
  And an idle song to sing
      Flaxen-Hair !

Shall I give you honesty
  Or lad's love to wear ?
Or a wreath less fair to see—
  Juniper and rosemary,
      Flaxen-Hair ?

Rosemary, lest you forget
  What was lief and fair :
Lad's love sweet thro' fear and fret,
Lad's love, green and living yet,
      Flaxen-Hair !

Phyllis and Damon

PHYLLIS and Damon met one day
    (Heigho!)
Phyllis was sad, and Damon gray,
Tired with treading a separate way.

Damon sighed for his broken flute :
    (Heigho!)
Phyllis went with a noiseless foot
Under the olives stript of fruit.

Met they, parted they, all unsaid?
    (Heigho!)
Ah! but a ghost's lips are not red ;
Damon was old and Phyllis dead.
    (Heigho!)

East o' the Sun and West o' the Moon

EAST o' the Sun, West o' the Moon,
There lies an island fair to see
Where Eld nor Autumn, any noon
Lay hands upon the blossomed tree :
Nor gold hair wears to sorry gray,
But youth is fain of endless May,
And yet, they say, love knows no rune
East o' the Sun, West o' the Moon.

It is an island lief and dear,
And they are sad who turn away
Their vessels from its sunshine clear
Into the mists of every-day.
And some there are that never come
In hearing of its winds that croon,
But vainly steer with longing dumb
East o' the Sun, West o' the Moon.

East o' the Sun are faces kind
That sorrow never turns away,
May's sunshine meets the April wind
Among the young green leaves at play.

There Greek and Trojan fight no more,
And Merlin sleeps upon the shore,
Leprechaun clouts Rhodope's shoon,
East o' the Sun, West o' the Moon.

There Eros seeks his shafts o'ersped
And Arne finds the flying tune,
There withered roses blossom red,
And Ariel's singing on the dune.
There in a castle strong, 'tis said,
Queen Brynhild dwells with white Gudrun—
And would my soul and thy soul sped
East o' the Sun, West o' the Moon.

I HAVE here to gratefully acknowledge the courtesy of the Editors of *The Yellow Book*, *The National Observer*, *Black and White*, *Sylvia*, and *The English Illustrated Magazine*, for permitting me to re-produce here divers poems which were originally published in their respective magazines.

PRINTED BY K. FOLKARD AND SON,
22, DEVONSHIRE STREET, QUEEN SQUARE, LONDON, W.C.